먼지별

도서출판 아시아에서는 《바이링궐 에디션 한국 대표 소설》을 기획하여 한국의 우수한 문학을 주제별로 엄선해 국내외 독자들에게 소개합니다. 이 기획은 국내외 우수한 번역가들이 참여하여 원작의 품격을 최대한 살렸습니다. 문학을 통해 아시아의 정체성과 가치를 살피는 데 주력해 온 도서출판 아시아는 한국인의 삶을 넓고 깊게 이해하는 데 이 기획이 기여하기를 기대합니다.

Asia Publishers presents some of the very best modern Korean literature to readers worldwide through its new Korean literature series 〈Bilingual Edition Modern Korean Literature〉. We are proud and happy to offer it in the most authoritative translation by renowned translators of Korean literature. We hope that this series helps to build solid bridges between citizens of the world and Koreans through a rich in-depth understanding of Korea.

바이링궐 에디션 한국 대표 소설 050

Bi-lingual Edition Modern Korean Literature 050

Dust Star

이경
먼지별

Lee Kyung

ASIA
PUBLISHERS

Contents

먼지별

Dust Star

"딱 3만 원어치만 가르쳐준다. 빵집 터는 법. 따라와."

열라 추운데 바람까지 지랄이다. 뭉텅이 먼지가 바지 자락을 잡고 북새질을 친다. 찌마가 영 말귀를 못 알아 듣는다. 고시원에서 쫓겨났다더니 제가 깔고 앉은 가방 속으로 처박히고 싶은 얼굴이다. 떠나기 전 얼굴이나 보고 가려고 골목 어귀에서 내내 기다렸다고, 날 보지 마자 혓바닥이 입 안에서 널브러진 소리를 냈다. 족히 몇 끼는 굶은 꼬락서니다. 뱃속을 외투처럼 열어볼 수 있다면 꼬불꼬불한 내장들이 기름기 하나 없이 밀가루 같은 먼지만 풀풀 날리고 있을 것이다. 지나가는 삐리 들한테 삥이나 뜯어서 컵라면이라도 먹여 보낼까 하다

"I'll teach you how to rob a bakery, but only thirty thousand *won*'s worth. Follow me!"

It was damn freezing; to top it all, the icy wind was a bitch. A cloud of dust was whirling around me, flapping and snapping at the hems of my pants. Chima had no clue about what I'd told him. He'd gotten kicked out of the *goshiwon* (cheap box-room lodging house), he'd told me, looking as if he wouldn't mind being crammed into the bag he'd been sitting on. He wanted to see my face before he took off, so he'd been waiting for me at the mouth of the alley. He'd hardly gotten the words out. Seemed he hadn't eaten for quite some time. If

그만두었다. 지금 가르쳐주지 않으면 오늘 밤 컵라면이 찌마의 마지막 끼니가 될지 모른다. 저 주변머리에 다른 데서 뭘 얻어먹는 건 죽어도 못한다. 빵집 터는 법을 알면 어디서든 굶어 죽진 않겠지. 몇 걸음 앞서 나가다 뒤를 돌아보니 찌마는 눈으로만 따라올 뿐 발바닥은 제자리를 뭉개고 있다.

"씨발, 추워 죽겠네. 마음 변하기 전에 빨리 와."

그제야 느릿느릿 움직이긴 하는데 마지못해 따라오는 빛이 역력하다. 빵집을 털기는커녕 먼지도 못 털겠다. 젠장, 집어치울까 울컥 치밀었지만 어차피 찌마에게 3만 원어치 뭐라도 해주긴 해줘야 한다.

"난 껌 한 통 훔쳐본 적이 없는데……."

거무튀튀한 피부에 검은자위를 둘러싼 흰자위만 도드라져 찌마의 눈동자는 유난히 캄캄하다. 모든 것이 캄캄했다는 점에서, 아빠와 닮았다. 노가다 판에서 근근이 연명하며 죽는 날까지 앞날이 캄캄하기만 했던 아빠였다. 언젠가 찌마에게 터무니없이 착해 보이는 그 눈은 바보로나 보인다고 티적거리자 벵갈인은 모두 같은 눈을 가졌다며 검은 창을 몇 번 열었다 닫았다 했다.

"빵집을 턴다는 말이 거슬리면 그럼 빵을 구한다는

you were to open his belly like an overcoat, you might see his empty, dust-covered intestines all twisted up without a hint of fat in them. It occurred to me that I could scrape some dough off some bums and buy Chima a cup-noodle or something. But I decided not to. If I didn't teach him today, the cup-noodle might very well be his last meal on earth. The way he was, he would never be able to beg for food. If he knew how to rob a bakery, he wouldn't be starving to death, at the least. Taking several steps ahead of him, I turned around and found him still standing in the same spot, following me only with his eyes.

"Damn it! I'm freezing to death here. Move it, before I change my mind."

It was only then that he began to move, slowly and, obviously, reluctantly. The way he was acting he wouldn't even be able to rob himself, let alone a bakery. 'Fuck it! Should I give it up?' But then I tried hard to stifle my anger. I was obliged to do something for him, something worthy of thirty thousand *won*.

"I've never even stolen a pack of gum..."

Chima's pupils seemed much darker in sharp contrast to the white of his eyes, which in turn

걸로 하면 되잖아."

"돈도 없이?"

"칼도 없이."

"칼을 들고 갈 생각은 정말 아니지?"

"그래. 돈도 없이 칼도 없이 빵을 구한다. 됐지? 자, 가자."

처음 집을 나올 때 나는 돈 대신 칼을 들고 나왔다. 열여섯 살 여자애가 주머니 속에 돈 대신 지녀야 할 것이 있다면 칼이었다. 칼은 책상 서랍 속에 있었다. 늘어진 수영복 같은 비키니 옷장의 지퍼를 열었을 때 동전 몇 개라도 눈에 띄었다면 서랍은 뒤지지 않았을지 모른다. 집을 나올 때마다 나는 매번 돌아갔다.

"아주 나가버리는 건 아니겠지."

며칠 전에도 노파는 가느스름히 눈을 뜨고 내 눈치를 살폈다. 그렇다고 거리로 나가는 날 잡지도 않았다. 거리가 노파를 먹여 살린다는 걸 안다. 노파는 앙상한 몸피를 방구석에 구긴 채 눈 가장자리에 눈물을 질금거렸다. 허구한 날 눈자위가 눅진눅진 젖어 있는 노파는 늙으니 오줌 지리듯이 괜한 눈물이 지려진다고 묻지도 않은 말을 옹잘거렸다.

stood out against his dark skin. He resembled my dad in that they both reminded me of darkness. A construction laborer living from hand to mouth, my dad had spent his life in darkness with absolutely no prospects until the day of his death. Once I'd teased Chima saying that his eyes looked too good-natured to the point of looking idiotic. He responded that all Bengalese have the same set of eyes. When he said that, he opened and closed his dark window-like eyes several times.

"If the expression 'rob a bakery' bothers you so much, then why don't we change it to 'get some bread'?"

"Without any money?"

"Without a knife."

"You don't mean to take a knife with you, do you?"

"Well, with no money, with no knife, we'll get some bread. All right? Now, let's go!"

When I left home for the first time, I took a knife, instead of money. It's a knife, not money, that a girl of sixteen should carry with her. I found the knife inside the desk drawer. Had I found some odd coins lying around inside that makeshift cloth-wardrobe when I opened its zipper, I wouldn't

"밥 채려놓구 가. 이년아."

노파는 허리가 기역 자로 굽기는 했어도 밥상을 못 차릴 정도는 아니다. 몇 달 만에 집에 들러도 봉지 속의 쌀을 야금야금 비워내며 질기게 살아 있었다. 물린 지 얼마 안 된 밥상이 버젓이 방 안에서 냄새를 피우고 있는데도 또 차려내라는 건 쌀이 얼마 남았나를 들여다보고 나가란 뜻이다. 오랜만에 들른 집이지만 옷만 갈아입고 돌아서는 길이었다. 봉지쌀은 벌써 부엌에 부려놓았다. 밀가루 봉지는 주둥이가 고무줄로 꽁꽁 묶인 채 찬장 구석에 있었다. 고무줄을 풀자 허연 가루가 풍 날렸다. 얼마간은 버틸 것이다.

"쉰 넘어 네년 낳느라고 짜부라졌다. 에밀 굶겨 죽이면 제명에 못 죽어."

노파는 쉰 살에 아빠를 만났다. 아무 데서나 치마를 들어올리던 술집 작부였다. 내가 여섯 살 무렵 저녁밥을 짓다 말고 집을 나갔다. 아빠 몰래 딱지를 뗐다방에 넘긴 후였다. 머잖아 일대가 개발된다는 소문을 듣고 집 한 칸이나마 갖고 있는 늙다리 총각에게 작정하고 꼬리를 쳤을 것이다. 마지막을 본 건 나였다.

엄마아. 대문을 열자 골목 끝을 벗어나는 엄마의 뒷모

have rummaged through the drawer. I left home more than once and each time, I returned.

'The girl isn't leaving for good this time, is she?' the old woman was studying my face, her eyes slightly opened. Nevertheless, she didn't stop me from leaving. The woman knew that the streets helped bring in food. Her body was crumpled up in the corner of the room, tears oozing out from the corners of her eyes. Her eyes were always wet and sticky with tears. Nobody asked her, but she grumbled and said things like, as you get older, tears leak out for no reason just like urine.

"Cook a meal for me before you take off, bitch!"

Although her back was stooped quite a bit, it wasn't so bad that she wasn't able to prepare a meal for herself. When I once came back after months of absence, I found the old woman keeping herself alive on one handful of rice a meal from a paper bag, just tenaciously hanging onto her dear life. Anyways, the old lady must have just eaten a meal: I could smell what was left over on the dining table right in the middle of the room. I realized that what she really wanted me to do was to take a look at the amount of rice left in the bag before I left. It had been a while since my last visit. Still, I

습이 보였다. 치맛자락에 바람이 들어 붕긋 부풀어서는 둥싯둥싯 떠나가고 있었다. 다시는 치마를 들어올리지 못하게 하겠다고 아빠가 몇 번이나 찢어놓았던 캉캉 치마였다. 다음날이면 감쪽같이 꿰매서 입던 그 치마를 입고 골목을 빠져나간 지 10여 년 만에 거지꼴에 반백이 되어 집이라고 기어 들어왔다. 1년 전이었다. 노파를 보자마자 아빠는 그 자리에 쓰러졌다. 한자리에 너무 오래 서 있었다는 듯이 픽. 심장 쇼크였다. 집을 날리고 다 허물어져가는 셋집으로 이사를 간 후에도 아빠는 한동안 살던 동네로 찾아가 엄마가 빠져나간 골목 끝에 의자를 놓고 앉아 있곤 했다.

장례를 치르는 내내 노파는 친척들 앞에서 목 놓아 울었다. 노파의 눈에서 마스카라가 검게 번져나왔다. 노파는 장례를 치르면서도 습관처럼 화장을 했다. 내 눈과 마주치자 손등으로 눈두덩을 훔쳐냈다. 마스카라가 뺨 전체로 흉하게 번졌다. 알지 못한 사정이 있지 않았겠냐. 이제라도 엄마 의지하면서 살아야 안 되겠냐. 일가 중의 누군가가 날 타일렀다. 심장이 굳은 것은 아빠만이 아니었다. 나는 언제라도 노파를 버릴 수 있었다.

wasn't going to stay long and was already on my way out after changing into fresh clothes. She didn't need to worry since I'd already bought a pack of rice and put it in the kitchen. I found a bag of flour with a length of elastic string tightly fastened around its pursed mouth in the corner of the cupboard. As soon as I undid the string and looked in, the bag belched a cloud of white flour. 'Well, she'll at least eke out her life for a little while.'

"I gave birth to you bitch when I was over fifty. That did a number on me. You won't be able to live out your own natural life if you let me die of hunger."

The old woman met my dad when she was fifty. She was a hostess at some random joint and ready to take off her skirt for anyone anywhere. She walked out on me—I was only six then—in the middle of cooking dinner. We were living in a house in the outskirts of Hwaseong City. One day, my family was given a so-called "residence permit" that would allow us to move into a suite in an apartment building that was to be built on the piece of land that my family house was a part of. By the time the woman ran away, she had already sold the permit to one of the "on-the-fly" real-estate agents

"밥 달래지 마. 다신 안 와."

노파는 내 말을 귓등으로 흘렸다. 뱃가죽이 등에 달라붙어 있는 노파가 떠오를 때쯤 어쩔 수 없이 나는 돌아갈 것이다. 굶어 죽을 뻔했다. 이년아. 노파는 손 갈퀴로 쌀 봉지를 채 갈 것이다.

나는 매일 밤 재워줄 사람을 찾아 공단 지대로 갔다. 공단 일대는 1톤 트럭들이 먼지를 날리며 좁은 도로 위에 앞바퀴 둘 뒷바퀴 넷을 아슬아슬 올려놓고 기우뚱 기울어져 지나다녔다. 바퀴가 지날 때마다 풀썩 일어나는 먼지가 가라앉을 틈이 없다. 비 오는 날이면 바큇자국을 따라 시커먼 물줄기가 흐르곤 했다. 논과 밭이 양쪽으로 늘어서 있는 비포장 길을 따라 커다란 텐트나 가건물이 드문드문 들어서 있는 공단 안으로 들어가면 알루미늄 새시를 조립하거나 용접에 매달려 있는 외국인들을 쉽게 볼 수 있다. 그들은 온 힘을 팔뚝과 다리에 모아 알루미늄 새시에 매달려 있었다. 팔과 다리만 있는 것 같은 사람들을 물끄러미 바라보고 있자면 어딘가 떨어져 있을 몸통이나 머리 같은 것을 주워다 조립해주고 싶어졌다. 주로 방글라데시, 파키스탄, 인도네시아 등지에서 온 무슬림들이었다. 화성 시내에 있는 모스크

in the area. Having heard the rumor about the land development plan for the area, she must have deliberately approached an aged bachelor.

It was me who saw her last. "Mommy!" I called out to her when I opened the front gate and caught a glimpse of her back as she fled the alley.

She seemed to be skidding along with her skirt ballooned out by the wind. It was the cancan skirt that Dad had ripped several times, saying that she was not to hold up that skirt ever again for another man. The ripped skirt would always be sewed back to its original shape the very next day. Ten odd years later, she came back gray-haired and shabby. That was last year.

Dad collapsed at the sight of the old woman, as if to say he had been staying in one place for far too long. He had heart attack. For some time, even after we lost the family house and the two of us moved into a run-down tenement, Dad would go to the old neighborhood and sit on a chair at the end of the alley where the woman had last been seen.

All through the funeral, the old woman wailed in front of our relatives. Black tears were flowing down from her heavily mascaraed eyes. She made

에 모여 인샬라, 샬롬 같은 말을 중얼거리는 금요일이 되면 그제야 팔, 다리, 머리가 제대로 끼워 맞춰진 사람으로 보였다.

공단 주위를 어슬렁거리다 야산 주변에 버려진 공터에 앉아 있으면 일을 마치고 돌아가는 외국인 노동자 한 명쯤 건지기는 식은 죽 먹기다. 어제는 인도네시아인과, 그저께는 방글라데시인과 잤다. 누구와 자도 상관없지만 그래도 외국인 쪽이 낫다. 외국인과 나란히 누우면 구질구질한 이 도시를 잠시라도 떠나 있는 기분이 들기 때문이다. 파키스탄인과 방글라데시인과 인도네시아인은 돌아가면서 날 재워주고 나는 매일 바지를 벗는다.

어젯밤 인도네시아인이 날 데려간 곳은 비닐하우스였다. 비닐하우스 안은 그럭저럭 집이라고 할만 했다. 플라스틱 3단 서랍장 안에 그릇과 옷이 차곡차곡 포개져 있었다. 때에 전 매트리스 위에 누워 인도네시아인은 밤새도록 자카르타에 있는 자기 집 이야기를 했다. 냄비 안에는 언제라도 먹을 수 있는 음식이 있고, 속옷이건 비누건 필요한 건 모두 제자리에 있는 곳이라고 했다. 뭐든지 거저 집어와도 되는 편의점에 관한 이야

her face, perhaps out of habit, even for the funeral. When our eyes met, she wiped her eyes with the back of her hand, smearing mascara all over her cheeks. "She must have had some reasons that we don't know about. It may not be too late to have Mother to rely on," one of the relatives tried to persuade me. Dad was not the only one with a hardened heart. I could always ditch the old woman whenever I wanted to.

"Don't you dare ask for rice. I'm not coming back!"

The woman turned a deaf ear to what I'd just said. I'd probably be back again when the image of a starving old woman, the skin of her belly hollowing in towards her back, happened to conjure itself up in my mind. "I nearly died of starvation, you bitch!" she would say as she snatched the bag of rice from me with her claws.

Every night, I went to the industrial complex looking for a person who would take me in for the night. I could always see, around the complex, one-ton trucks passing by with their bodies tilted, their two front wheels and four back wheels dangerously perched on the shoulders of narrow roads, stirring up clouds of dust as they went by.

기를 듣고 있는 것 같았다. 곁에 누운 인도네시아인이 먼 곳의 집을 더듬을 때 나는 비닐하우스 위에서 돌고 있을 화성을 떠올렸다.

처음 찌마에게서 화성이라는 별이 오렌지색 먼지로 뒤덮여 있다는 말을 들었을 때 내겐 그게 너무나 당연한 일처럼 여겨졌다. 화성이라는 이름만 들어도 먼지가 풀썩이는 것 같으니까. 어쩌면 먼지별 화성과 지상의 화성은 먼지에 가려 서로를 알아보지 못하는 쌍둥이인지도 모른다.

언젠가 찌마에게 왜 집을 떠나왔느냐고 했더니 빵을 찾아서 왔다고 했다. 원래 길이란 것은 빵을 구하려고 만든 것이라면서, 인간은 언제나 빵을 찾아서 가기 마련이고, 자기도 파키스탄에서 대학까지 나왔지만 결국 여기까지 흘러오게 되었다고 했다. 그곳에서 취직을 해볼 곳이라고는 이슬라마바드나 카라치에 있는 직물공장 정도였는데, 너도나도 몰려드는 통에 취직할 엄두도 못 냈거니와 월급도 형편없었다고 했다. 빤한 얘기였다. 일자리를 찾아 행성처럼 떠돌다 이곳에 불시착한 거였다. 마땅하게 착륙할 곳이 없어 거리를 떠돌다 아무 데서나 바지를 벗는 나처럼 말이다. 먼지 속에서 기

One truck after another, there was no time for the dust to settle. On rainy days, black streams of water flowed along the ruts. I walked along the unpaved road flanked by rice paddies and fields on either side and entered the complex. It was sparsely dotted by large tents and makeshift buildings. I always found foreign workers assembling aluminum window parts or working on welding jobs there. They all seemed to channel all their strength into their arms and legs in order to hang onto the aluminum parts. They looked like their bodies were composed of only arms and legs. I wanted to pick up their torsos and heads lying somewhere and assemble them back together. The majority of them were Muslims from Bangladesh, Pakistan, Indonesia, etc. On Fridays, they went to their mosque downtown in Hwaseong City and mumbled expressions like "Inshallah" or "Shalom." Only there did they look like real humans with arms, legs, and heads attached to where they were supposed to be.

I wandered around the complex, and sat in the abandoned clearing near the hill. It was a piece of cake to meet one of the foreign workers on their way back to their homes after work. Yesterday, I

침을 뱉으며 찌마가 말했다.

"한국으로 가려고 말을 배우고는 있었지만 막상 집을 떠나려니까 쉽지 않았어. 무섭기도 하고 막막하기도 하고. 화성이라는 도시가 한국말로 태양계의 네 번째 행성과 발음이 같다는 걸 알았을 때 비행기를 탈 용기가 생겼어. 어쩐지 지상에서는 찾을 수 없는 것들이 찾아질 것 같았거든."

화성. 살아나가기 위해 온몸으로 바닥을 밀고 나가지 않아도 되는 곳. 얼빠지게 살아도 살아지는 곳. 노파의 폭삭 굽은 허리로는 올려다볼 수 없는 곳. 찌마와 나는 지상의 화성에 잘못 버려진 거였다. 언젠가는 오렌지색 먼지 폭풍을 타고 진짜 화성으로 날아가고 싶었다.

나는 밤의 어디쯤에서 화성을 본 적이 있었다. 내리 세 끼를 굶었더니 하늘과 땅이 한데 엉겨버린 검은 덩어리 속에서 허우적대는 것 같았다. 잠자리는 지하도나 건물의 계단에서 해결했지만 당장 배를 채우는 게 급했다. 주머니 속의 칼은 만일의 위험에 대비하기 위한 것이었지 그것으로 돈을 구할 엄두는 나지 않았다. 작정하고 나온 것도 아니어서 아르바이트 할 자리도 없었다. 신원보증을 서줄 사람이 없으면 일자리 구하기가

slept with an Indonesian and the day before, with a Bangladeshi. It didn't matter who I slept with. Even so, I preferred foreigners, because when I was lying side by side with a foreigner I felt I was in a place that was, if however briefly, far away from this dreary city. The Pakistani, Bangladeshi, and Indonesian took turns providing me with a place to sleep and each night, I took off my pants.

Last night, an Indonesian took me to a vinyl house. It wasn't so bad inside; one could even call it a house. There was tableware and clothes stacked neatly in a plastic chest of drawers. As he lay on his soiled mattress, the Indonesian talked about his home in Jakarta all night. According to the Indonesian, there was always something to eat in the pot in Indonesia; and underwear, soap, toothpicks, and other necessities could always be found in their proper places. I felt as if I was listening to a story about a convenience store where you could take anything for free. While the Indonesian beside me groped for his faraway home, I was thinking about the planet Mars orbiting way beyond this vinyl house.

When I first heard from Chima that Mars is a star wrapped under a blanket of orange dust, I thought

하늘의 별 따기라는 건 나중에야 알았다.

공단 지대로 접어드는 큰길을 따라 사거리 길 모퉁이까지 왔을 때였다. 크고 둥그런 빛이 주위를 환한 오렌지색으로 물들이고 있었다. 먼지가 금박지처럼 반짝반짝 떠다니고 있었다. 화성빵집에서 흘러나오는 오렌지색 조명이었다. 나는 홀린 것처럼 빛 속으로 걸어 들어가 빵집 안을 들여다봤다. 천장과 벽이 온통 푸른색으로 칠해져 있고 별처럼 빵이 둥둥 떠다니고 있었다. 은하수는 바게트였고 국자 모양의 북두칠성은 도넛 일곱 개였다. 태양 모양의 케이크 주위로 크림빵과 단팥빵이 위성처럼 돌고 있었다. 오렌지색 할로겐 등이 푸른 천장 위에서 샛별처럼 빛났다. 빵이 별처럼 빛나는 곳. 깨져 있기 십상인 가로등이 몇 개 흩어져 있을 뿐인 그곳에선 단연 일등성의 별빛이었다.

밤을 견뎌볼 셈으로 건물 안으로 들어갔다. 2층과 3층으로 통하는 문은 단단히 잠겨 있었다. 간판만 걸어놓았지 장사는 하질 않아 아예 문을 걸어놓은 것 같았다. 4층은 옥상이었다. 빈 종이박스들이 한구석에 쌓여 있었다. 박스를 바닥에 깔고 바람막이를 세워서 잠자리를 만들었다. 종이박스에서 빵 냄새가 맡아졌다.

it was only natural. The name Mars itself seemed to stir up dust in my mind. Perhaps, Mars, a star of dust, and Hwaseong on earth, are twins who can't recognize each other because they're both blinded by dust.[1] Once I asked Chima why he had left home; he said he had followed the bread crumbs. Roads were made to look for bread in the first place and humans were bound to move towards bread, he said. He was a university graduate from Pakistan. Nevertheless, he had ended up here. The best jobs available in his country were ones in textile factories in Islamabad or Karachi. But too many job seekers scrambled for those jobs, so he couldn't even dream of getting one of those. Besides, wages were terrible. No surprise there, I thought. He had been wandering around like a planet before he had crashed here. He was just like me: he had no decent place to land. I was wandering the streets and taking my pants off anywhere they would have me. Coughing in the dust, Chima told me:

"I was learning Korean so I could come to Korea, but leaving home was never easy. I felt uncertain and scared. When I heard that in Korean, the city's name Hwaseong was pronounced the same as that

"간단해. 빵집으로 걸어 들어가서 빵을 달라고 하면 되는 거야."

난 찌마가 죽어도 못하는 말이라는 걸 알면서 일부러 윽박질렀다. 고시원이 있는 골목 끝은 널찍한 공터와 이어져 있다. 올챙이묵이나 된장을 사발에 담아 파는 오일장이 꼬박꼬박 서는 공터엔 버려진 푸성귀 쪼가리들이 얼어서 버석버석 밟혔다. 그나마 어기적거리며 따라오던 찌마가 쓰레기 더미를 지근지근 밟고 섰다. 길 건너 공단 지대에는 성긴 불빛이 흐릿하다.

"날 새겠네."

새끼가 셔터 문을 내릴 시간이다. 문 닫기 직전이 손님이 가장 뜸하다. 사거리까지 가려면 서둘러야 한다. 언 땅을 퍽퍽 차며 찌마에게 다가가 다짜고짜 팔을 잡아끌었다. 찌마는 맥없이 끌려왔다.

사거리로 가는 길에는 얼마 전만 해도 미장원과 종묘상, 전파사 등이 듬성듬성 들어서 있었다. 오래된 가게의 낡은 벽면에는 언제 칠했는지도 모르는 페인트가 태연하게 빛바래 가고 있었다. 어느 날부턴지 가건물들이 우뚝우뚝 솟아나기 시작했다. 이불집, 인테리어집, 그럴듯하게 꾸며놓긴 했지만 장사를 위해 문을 여는 집은

of the fourth planet of the solar system, I was able to muster up all my courage to get on the plane. I thought I would be able to find things that were impossible to find here on the earth."

'Mars—where you don't need to hustle on the bottom with all your might in order to survive, where you don't have to be always up to your tricks to feed yourself, which the eyes of the deeply stooped old woman cannot reach.' Chima and I had been by mistake abandoned on the earthly Mars. I wished someday I'd get swept up by a dust storm and carried off to the real Mars.

I had seen Mars somewhere in the dark. After missing three meals, I felt that I was struggling in the black mass of the sky and land melting into each other. I could always sleep in the under-ground pass or staircase of a building if I wanted to. But hunger was another matter. The knife in my pocket was for protection. I didn't dare to use it to take money from someone. I left home with no fu ture plans at all, not even the prospect of a part-time job. I realized belatedly that it was impossible to get a job without a reference.

I walked along the main road leading to the in-dustrial complex. When I came to a corner of an

없다. 개발이 시작되면 나올 상가 딱지를 노리고 지은 가건물들이다. 이 거리엔 흔한 게 이런 불 꺼진 집이다. 허술한 문을 따고 들어가 잘 만한 곳도 몇 군데 봐두었다. 당장 오늘 밤부터가 걱정이다. 찌마가 거기까지 생각해두었을 리가 없다.

찌마는 파키스탄을 떠나와 5년이 지나도록 그 흔한 비닐하우스나 컨테이너 박스 하나 구하지 못했다. 찌마의 집은 고시원이었다. 말이 고시원이지, 부랑자나 노숙자 처지가 되기 직전의, 마지막 남은 돈을 거기에다 조금씩 흘려 넣고 있는 치들이 대부분이었다. 여기저기 전전하다 짐 가방이라도 겨우 부려놓은 곳이 고시원이었는데 오늘 밤 그마저 돈이 떨어져 쫓겨난 것이었다.

처음 만난 날도 찌마는 바람 빠진 풍선처럼 너덜너덜해 보였다. 그날은 낮부터 공단 근처를 싸돌아다녔는데도 한 놈도 걸리지 않았다. 재워줄 사람을 못 찾은 빔이면 공단 지대 맞은편 주택가로 들어갔다. 낡은 여관을 개조한 고시원과 하숙집, 허름한 여인숙이 줄지어 서 있는 골목에 피시방이 있었다. 인터넷도 제대로 되지 않는, 나 같은 애들이 한동안 머물 수 있는 곳이다. 피시방 근처로 오긴 했는데 거기 들어갈 돈도 없었다. 골목

intersection, I saw a large circle of light tinge the surroundings with orange color. Glistening dust particles were floating in the light. It was the orange illumination of Hwaseong Bakery. I walked into the light as if bewitched. The walls and ceiling inside were painted blue all over. Bread and bun samples were hanging from the ceiling and floating like stars. The Milky Way was made up of baguettes. The Great Dipper had been fashioned using seven doughnuts. Cream buns and red bean jam buns were orbiting like satellites around a sun-shaped cake. The orange light shone from the ceiling like the morning star. It was a place where buns twinkled like stars. That orange light was definitely the brightest star in an area illuminated only by street lamps, most of which were very likely broken. I entered the building hoping to stay the night there. The doors to the second and third floor were locked; perhaps the business wasn't good enough to keep those doors open. The forth floor was the rooftop. Empty boxes were stacked up in one corner. I prepared to sleep by putting a flattened box on the floor and the other boxes stacked up around it to block the wind. The boxes smelled like bread.

끝에서 걸어나오는 시커먼 사내가 있기에 한번 찔러보았다.

"아저씨, 할래요? 100원어치도 해드려요."

그가 눈을 껌벅이자 밤의 창문이 열리는 것 같았다. 나보다 머리 세 개는 더 큰 키를 구부정하게 굽히고 내려다보더니 말없이 주머니를 뒤적여 돈을 꺼냈다. 2만 원이었다. 아직 지폐를 구분 못하나 싶어서 한 번 더 찔러보았다.

"아저씨, 공정거래가 3만 원이야."

찌마는 말없이 주머니에서 만 원짜리 한 장을 더 꺼내주었다. 그리고 가던 길을 갔다. 나는 순간적으로 어리벙벙해졌다. 돈을 주면 뭐든지 가질 수 있고, 뭐든 가지려면 돈을 주어야 한다는 원칙은 가위바위보 같은 것이다. 가위바위보를 모르는 사람과 가위바위보를 할 수 없듯이, 돈을 주고도 멍청하게 아무것도 달라지 않는 그에게 나는 무엇을 해주어야 할지 잠시 잊어버렸다. 무작정 그를 따라갔다. 3만 원어치 뭐든 해주어야 할 것 같아서였다. 허술한 입성에 허적허적 걸어가는 걸음새를 보자 슬슬 3만 원이나 뺏은 게 켕기기 시작하는데, 그가 어느 건물 안으로 들어가는 게 보였다. 건물 안으

32

"It's simple. You just walk in the bakery and ask for bread. That's all!"

I threatened him on purpose. I knew very well that he could never speak those words. The *goshiwon* alley was connected to a large clearing, an area for an outdoor market opening every five days. You could buy tadpole jelly or fermented bean paste by the bowl. But now it was deserted, nothing left but wasted frozen vegetable crushing under our feet as we walked on it. Chima, who had been reluctantly following along, stopped walking altogether on top of a pile of garbage. The industrial complex on the other side of the street was dimly lit with a handful of lamps. It would soon be too late. The bakery owner would shortly take down the shutters for the night. Usually, few customers were there around the closing time. We had to hurry to make it to the intersection in time. I walked up to Chima, kicking the frozen ground as I approached. Without saying anything, I grabbed hold of his arm and pulled. This time, he didn't put up any resistance.

Until recently, the street leading to the intersection used to have shops, if only sparsely, like a hair saloon, a nursery, a home electric appliance shop,

로 사라진 지 몇 분 후에 다시 나와서 편의점으로 들어갔다. 소주 한 병을 사가지고 나온 찌마는 골목에 선 채로 병나발을 불었다. 나는 잠시 망설이다가 과자 한 봉지를 사와서 내밀었다.

"공짜로 뭘 주는 건 처음이야. 나한테 공짜로 뭘 준 것도 니가 처음이고."

찌마는 받지 못한 석 달 치 월급 중에 한 달분을 받은 날이라서 한 병 까는 중이라고 했다. 사장이 거래처에서 모처럼 수금을 해 와 기분이 좋았는지 선심 쓰듯이 내주었다고 했다. 고시원에서는 술은 못 하게 되어 있다며 멋쩍게 웃었다. 술병을 든 그의 오른손이 보일락 말락 떨렸다.

잠자리를 구하지 못한 밤이면 찌마의 방으로 숨어들어갔다. 찌마는 바지를 벗기지 않고도 재워주었다. 잠을 재워주는 대신 비지를 빚겠냐고 했더니, 그냥 벗고 싶다면 몰라도 재워주는 대신으로는 싫다고 했다. 벗으면 벗는 거지 무슨 차이가 있느냐고 하면서 바지 지퍼를 내리려는데 허둥지둥 지퍼를 다시 올려주며 너무나 커서 도저히 말로는 다 설명할 수 없는 차이가 있다고 했다. 나로서는, 재워주는 대신으로는 바지를 벗을 수

and so on. The paint on the walls—who knows when the walls had first been painted—outside some of the old shops had been quietly fading away. Then, new makeshift structures began to spring up in place of the old shops: a quilt shop, an interior design store, etc. They looked okay, but none of them had been open for business. They were make-believe structures with the aim of obtaining commercial permits once land development began in the area. The street was full of shops of this type, shops with dark windows. I'd eyed a few of these places that I could easily break into in order to spend the night, including that night. I didn't think Chima could have managed to plan that far ahead.

Since his departure from Pakistan, Chima hadn't been able to get even one of those easy-to-get vinyl houses or container boxes for five years. Chima had been living in one of the *goshiwons* in the area. The *goshiwon* didn't even deserve its name; it was full of people on the brink of becoming street bums or homeless, people trickling whatever money they still had left into their rent. He had been moving around from one place to another before he came to the *goshiwon*. But that night, he hadn't

있지만 어쩐지 그냥은 벗을 수 없었다. 흔들리는 그의 눈을 보자 아빠 앞에서 바지를 내리는 기분이 들었던 것이다. 아빠의 눈은 종종 까닭 없이 흔들리곤 했다. 불안하기 때문이라고 했다. 살아 있기 때문에 살아갈 일이 불안한 아빠였다. 죽어버린 아빠는 지금쯤 차라리 속이 편할지도 모른다.

그날 밤 내내 그는 꼭 물린 지퍼처럼 입을 꾹 다물어버렸다. 넬모레면 마흔이 가까운 주제에 꽤 순정파다. 미나리 싹 같은 나와 진짜 연애질이라도 하자는 건가. 나는 진짜 연애 같은 건 싫다. 조건 없이 주기만 하는 사랑이란 건 대체 뭘 얼마큼 주어야 하는지 가늠할 수 없다. 게다가 정말 사랑이라도 하게 되면 다른 외국인들과 자기 싫어질 것 같았다. 매일 찌마와 자느냐, 다른 외국인과 자느냐를 선택하라고 한다면 생각할 것도 없었다. 찌마는 제 입에 넣을 빵 한쪽 못 구한다.

그는 일하던 알루미늄 공장이 문을 닫자 다른 직장을 구하지 못했다. 안 그래도 키만 멀쩡하게 컸지 손재주도 없고 굼뜬 데다 주변머리까지 없으니 사나흘만 일해도 공장주들은 마뜩잖은 기색을 보이곤 했다. 게다가 알루미늄 기둥에 손목이 깔리는 사고를 당한 이후로 오

been able to even pay for lodging in the *goshiwon* and had been kicked out.

Even the night I first met him, he looked as ragged as a burst balloon. That day, I began to hang around the complex even before nightfall. But I couldn't get anyone to take me in for the night. Nights like that, I usually went to the residential area opposite the complex. There was a PC game room in an alley lined with old inn-turned-*goshiwons*, boarding houses, and cheap inns. The PC-game room didn't even have Internet access, but it was perfect for kids like myself to stay for a while. I came to the game room, but had no money to get in. A man with dark skin was leaving the back end of the alley. I decided to give it a shot.

"Hey, Mister, you wanna do it? I can even do a hundred *won*'s worth."

He blinked his eyes, which made me feel as though the window of the night had been opened. He was three heads taller than me. He stooped down to look at my face. Silently, he took some money out of his pocket. Twenty thousand *won*. 'Perhaps, he didn't even know the value of Korean paper money?' I thought and tried another shot at it.

"Mister, the going price for a woman is thirty

른손을 떨게 되자 화성 일대에서 찌마를 받아주는 곳은 없었다. 어쩌다 일자리를 잡아도 오래가지 못했다. 공장주들은 이런저런 핑계를 대며 몇 달 치 월급을 미루다 핑곗거리가 떨어지면 나가라고 했다. 사소한 트집에도 찌마는 여지없이 쫓겨났다. 그렇다고 파키스탄으로 돌아갈 수도 없었다. 파키스탄을 떠나올 때 브로커에게 들인 돈이 고스란히 빚으로 남아서 그 돈을 갚기 전에는 어찌해볼 도리가 없었다. 찌마는 오도 가도 못하고 화성을 맴돌 수밖에 없었다.

불 꺼진 가건물들이 줄지어 서 있는 야트막한 경사로를 찌마를 끌다시피 해서 넘어가자니 슬그머니 부아가 치민다. 휙 돌아서 찌마를 눈으로 잡아끌었다. 찌마가 밤의 창문을 열고 물끄러미 날 내려다보았다. 저런 눈을 하면 어쩔 줄 모르겠다. 뭘 어쩌라는 건지도 모르겠고.

"너더러 구걸을 하라는 게 아니야. 빵을 달라고 하라니까. 그건 나쁜 게 아냐. 누구나 배는 고프니까."

빵집 옥상에서 밤을 새운 후 별수 없이 집으로 돌아갔지만 며칠 후 다시 나왔다. 노파와 마주 보고 손가락이나 빨아봤자 뾰족한 수가 없기는 마찬가지였다. 거리 쪽이 백배는 속 편했다. 밤이 오면 나는 사거리 모퉁이

thousand *won*."

Chima, still silent, took out another bill from his pocket. Then he began to walk away. I was dumb-founded. There are principles when using money, like playing rock-paper-scissors. With enough money you can get whatever you want, but once you pay for it, you have the right to demand it. You can't play rock-paper-scissors with someone who doesn't know the rules, though.

So I was at quite a loss, not knowing what to do with a man who didn't demand anything in ex-change for his money. I just followed after him, feeling that I needed to do something worth thirty thousand *won*. His shabby clothes and the way he shuffled made me feel guilty about hustling that much money from him. He went in a building and came out a few minutes later. Then he entered a convenience store, came out with a bottle of li-quor, and began drinking from the bottle as he stood in the alley. I hesitated awhile, but in the end, I bought a bag of cookies and held it out to him.

"This is the first time I've ever given away any-thing for free. Also, you're the first person who's ever given me anything for free."

Chima said that he just got paid a month's salary

를 찾아갔다. 오렌지색 먼지별을 올려다보면 마음이 놓였다. 그 안에는 언제라도 빵이 있으니까. 아직 편의점을 털지도, 외국인과 잘 줄도 몰랐던 나는 여전히 배가 고팠다. 외국인 한 명이 빵집으로 들어가는 게 보였다. 입구 쪽 카운터에는 주인 남자가 혼자서 장부를 정리하고 있었다. 외국인은 빵이 있는 쪽은 쳐다보지도 않고 곧바로 남자에게로 걸어갔다. 다짜고짜 쿠브즈를 내놓으라고 했다. 나중에 공단 지역에서 만난 터키인에게 물어보니 쿠브즈는 주로 아랍의 무슬림들이 먹는 식빵이라고 했다. 그 빵집은 화성의 외국인들에게는 소문난 곳이었다. 밀가루 반죽에 효모와 소금을 넣어서 엉성하게 내놓은 쿠브즈가 입소문을 타기 시작하자 남자는 타노우르라는 화덕을 만들어놓고 진짜 쿠브즈를 구워내기 시작했다. 쿠브즈뿐만이 아니라 차파티라든가 로티라든가 이름도 못 들어본 외국인들의 빵을 재주껏 구워 팔았다. 외국인은 쿠브즈를 내놓으라고 막무가내로 남자를 다그쳤다. 빵을 달라거나 팔라는 것이 아니었다. 그냥 가져가겠다는 거였다. 잠시 맡겨 놓은 개라도 돌려달라는 태도였다. 쇼윈도 너머에서 지켜보고 있는 나조차도 어이가 없었다. 주인 남자가 상대의 뱃속이 훤

out of three months in arrears and that he was celebrating with the bottle. His boss was in a generous mood that day and had paid him without any fuss. Perhaps, he continued, his boss had somehow been able to collect some money from his clients. He added that he was not allowed to drink in the *goshiwon*. He smiled awkwardly. Then I saw his right hand that held the bottle shaking slightly.

Whenever I was out of luck finding a place to sleep, I snuck into Chima's room. Chima let me stay the night without taking off my pants. Once I suggested I pay for the room by taking off my pants. But he said if I really wanted to take them off, he wouldn't mind, but not in return for the room. I started to unzip my pants, saying that there was no difference between the two. But he hurriedly zipped them up himself and said the difference was so great that he couldn't possibly explain it in words. As for me, I was willing to take off my pants to pay for the room, but I couldn't do it otherwise. Detecting a stir in his eyes, I felt as if I was doing it in front of my dad. I had often found an inexplicable stir in Dad's eyes. He said it was because he was anxious. Because he was alive, he felt uneasy about making a living. Dad might be feeling better

41

히 보인다는 투로 말했다.

"돈은 내놔야지."

외국인이 가슴팍에서 뭔가를 번쩍 빼 들었다. 초승달 모양의 단검이었다. 칼은 천장에 그려진 별과 묘하게 잘 어울렸다.

"우린 지금 라마단 기간 중이다. 벌써 보름째 해가 지기 전엔 아무것도 못 먹고 있다. 무슬림들에겐 자카트의 의무란 것이 있다. 배고픈 사람에게 빵을 주어야 하는 의무다. 넌 자카트는 고사하고 율법으로 금하는 이자놀이를 하면서 형제들을 신고해 잡아가게 했다. 무슬림들에겐 그런 놈들을 위한 의무가 한 가지 더 있다. 악을 응징하는 지하드의 의무. 네가 빵을 내놓고 자카트를 행하겠나? 내가 지하드를 행할까?"

화성빵집은 빵으로만 유명한 곳이 아니었다. 주인 남자는 외국인들에게 여권을 담보로 맡고 터무니없는 이자로 돈을 빌려주었다. 무슬림들은 고리대금업을 죄악시한다지만 화성에서 돈을 빌려주는 곳은 그나마 빵집밖에 없어서 외국인들은 그곳을 드나들 수밖에 없었다. 그들은 공장에서 도망칠 수는 있어도 빵집으로부터는 도망칠 수 없었다. 여권 때문이었다. 하루라도 이자를

now in that he had stopped living.

All through that night, Chima kept his mouth zipped up. He was quite naive for a man pushing forty. Was he saying that he and I, as young as I was, should have a real love affair? I hate real love affairs. With so-called unconditional love, I would never figure out what and how much I should give. Further, if I were in love with someone, I wouldn't like to sleep with other foreigners. Given a choice between sleeping with Chima every night and sleeping with different foreigners, I wouldn't hesitate in choosing the latter. Chima was unable to feed even himself.

After the aluminum factory where he used to work went under, he couldn't get another job. This giant man had no practical skills to show of. Making it worse, he was slow at work and had no tact. After three, or four days of work, his employers would have enough of him already.

To top it all off, he had had an accident where an aluminum beam had fallen on his wrist. After the accident, his right hand became shaky and no one in the Hwaseong area would hire him. Even when he managed to get a job, it didn't last long. His employers would make excuses for delaying his pay-

늦게 내거나 제날짜에 나타나지 않으면 남자는 출입국 관리소에 불법체류자로 신고해버렸다. 단속에 걸려서 여권이 확인되지 않으면 강제출국을 당하기 때문에 외국인들은 대부분 제 발로 빵집을 찾아갔다. 불법체류자 신분이 된 다음에도 빵집을 벗어날 수 없기는 마찬가지였다. 강제출국을 당하려고 해도 여권이 없으면 외국인 보호소에 반년이고 1년이고 발이 묶이기 십상이어서, 어차피 빵집으로 돌아오기 마련이었다.

외국인은 한 치의 틈도 주지 않고 주인 남자를 쏘아보았다. 주인 남자도 물러서지 않고 외국인을 노려보았다. 당장이라도 초승달이 주인 남자의 가슴팍에 꽂힐 것 같아서 나는 눈을 질끈 감았다. 주인 남자가 말했다.

"갖고 꺼져. 다시 오면 국물도 없을 줄 알아. 어쨌든 무슬림들 때문에 장사를 하고 있으니까 이번만은 봐주는 거야. 알라가 뭐라고 했건 내 알 바 아니야. 화성빵집에선 내가 알라야."

외국인은 가소롭다는 듯이 인샬라라는 말을 남기고 서둘러 빵집을 빠져나왔다. 창문 밖에서 기웃거리던 나는 외국인에게 얼른 길을 비켜주었다. 인샬라, 인샬라. 뜻도 모르는 인사를 외국인의 꽁무니에 대고 중얼거렸

ments for several months. When they ran out of excuses, they would lay him off. For any number of trivial reasons, Chima would be laid off again.

He couldn't go back to Pakistan, either. Because of his debts—the money he had borrowed to pay the broker who'd arranged his move to Korea, he couldn't go back before he paid it off. Chima had no choice but to hang around Hwaseong.

While almost pulling Chima along the easy slope lined with unlit makeshift buildings, I felt anger bubbling up inside myself. I quickly turned around and pulled him with my eyes. Chima opened his windows of the night and looked down at me. I never knew what to do whenever he gave me that look. What was he expecting me to do? But I didn't avert my eyes from his. Like him, I didn't even have a vinyl house to sneak into.

"I'm not asking you to beg. Just demand some bread. That's not so bad. Everybody gets hungry."

Having spent a night awake on the rooftop of the bakery, I went back home. But a few days later, I was on the street again. Things were not different at home: it wouldn't do anybody any good just looking at each other, feeling hungry and sorry for ourselves. At least on the street, I felt much more

45

다. 빵을 주어야 하는 의무. 사람들은 나 같은 애한테 빵을 주어야 하는 의무가 있다지 않은가. 그 말은 어디 한 군데 비빌 곳 없는 내게 말이 아니라 언덕이었다. 돈 대신에 칼을 들이밀 때 나는 지갑 속을 뒤져내듯 그 말을 찾아내곤 했다. 화성빵집은 머릿속에 그려왔던 진짜 화성과는 거리가 멀었지만, 언제든지 마음만 먹으면 빵을 얻는 방법을 알려주었다는 점에서 여전히 내게는 빛나는 행성이었다.

내가 빵집을 터는 방법은 그 외국인과는 조금 달랐다. 태연하게 빵집 문을 열고 들어가는 것까지는 같았다. 나는 빵을 달라고 말하는 대신 침착하게 진열대로 가서 빵을 집었다. 절대로 세 개 이상은 집지 않았다. 눈치를 챈 주인이 무슨 짓이냐고 소리를 치면 똑바로 노려보면서 칼을 뺀다. 초승달 모양이면 좋았겠지만 비키니 옷장에서 꺼낸 건 연필 깎을 때나 쓰는 커터 칼이었다. 엄지로 녹슨 칼날을 밀어올리면 찌르륵 소름 끼치는 소리가 났다. 여기까지 성공하면 다 된 거나 마찬가지다. 나 같은 애들은 무슨 짓이건 한다. 세상의 모든 빵집 주인들도 그 정도는 안다. 팽팽하게 당겨진 긴장의 끈을 한 번 더 감아쥐면서 서서히 뒷걸음질 쳐 나오면 되는

peaceful inside. At nightfall, I went to the corner of the intersection. Looking up at the orange light, I felt relaxed. There was always bread in the bakery. I had neither robbed any convenience store yet nor learned how to survive by sleeping with foreigners. And I was hungry as usual. I saw a foreigner go in the bakery. At the cashier's counter near the entrance of the store was the owner sitting alone and doing some bookkeeping. The foreigner didn't even turn to see the bread display, but went straight to the owner and demanded *kuvs*. Later, I asked a Turk I met on the complex and learned that *kuvs* is a kind of bread eaten mainly by Muslims in the Arab world. That bakery was well known to the foreigners in Hwaseong. As the news of the bread, rather sloppily baked out of a dough mixed with yeast and salt in that bakery, spread by word of mouth and became popular, the baker began to bake real *kuvs* in a stove called *tanour*. He produced not only *kuvs* but also other kinds of foreign bread to the best of his ability, bread with foreign-sounding names like *chapati* and *roti*.

That foreigner relentlessly pressed the baker for *kuvs*. It was obvious that he wasn't going to pay for it; he wanted it for free. It was as if he was picking

거였다. 대개의 경우 주인은 경찰을 부르거나 하진 않았다. 그래 봤자 빵 몇 개일 뿐이니까. 고래고래 지르는 빵집 주인의 고함을 뒤통수에 달고 모퉁이 몇 개를 꺾어 달려 나오면 끝이었다. 열흘이든 한 달이든 나는 거리에서 살아갈 수 있게 되었다.

"넌, 당당히 빵을 달라고 말하라지만, 말도, 안 돼. 누가 그냥, 빵을 주겠니? 내 처지를 몰라서, 그래……? 너와는, 달라."

찌마의 목소리가 뚝뚝 끊어졌다. 언덕을 오르느라 숨이 차서 그러는 것도 같고, 눈물을 억지로 삼키는 것도 같다. 나는 사납게 눈을 치떴다. 찌마는 입을 닫지 않았다.

"사, 사람들이, 내게 뭘 주어야 한다면…… 그건, 일자리야."

입으로 거저 들어오는 밥숟가락은 없다.

아빠는 밥상머리에서 식전기도처럼 주위섬기곤 했다. 아빠가 일을 나갈 수 없는 날이면 우리는 한 끼 밥을 걸렀다. 방문을 열면 코앞에 신발을 벗어놓는 자리가 부엌이었다. 어느 날은 하루를 공치고 방에 누워 있는 아빠 몰래 살금살금 부엌을 뒤졌다. 그릇 몇 개가 오른 허술한 밥상은 물리자마자 금세 배가 고팠다. 후다닥

up his own dog after leaving it in someone else's care for a brief while. I witnessed the whole scene through the window, and the foreigner's demands left even me dumbfounded. "Do you have money?" the baker asked in a tone deliberately betraying his knowledge of the foreigner's intention. The foreigner drew out something shiny from his chest. It was a dagger in the shape of crescent moon. Ironically, the dagger seemed to be in perfect harmony with the stars drawn on the ceiling.

"We are in the middle of Ramadan period. We haven't eaten anything before sunset for fifteen days. We haven't eaten anything all day today, either. We Muslims have an obligation called *zakat*, that is, an obligation to provide hungry people with food. You are not just violating *zakat*, but engaging in the forbidden practice of moneylending and even reporting my brothers to the police and getting them arrested. We have one more obligation to observe against your kind of people. It's called *jihad*, an obligation to punish the evil. Do you want to observe *zakat* by surrendering your bread? Or do you want me to execute *jihad* on you?"

Hwaseong bakery was not only widely known for its bread, but also for the owner's shady deals with

밥 한 숟가락을 입에 넣고 물을 마시려는데 벌컥 미닫
이문이 열렸다. 그냥 노는 게 영 불안했던지 아빠 손엔
연장 가방이 들린 채였다. 미안하기도 하고 당황하기도
해서 잽싸게 밥그릇을 등 뒤로 돌린다는 게 그만 엎어
버렸다. 밥그릇이 수챗구멍 가로 굴렀다. 허연 젖가슴
같은 밥덩이가 시멘트 바닥에 동그마니 솟았다. 아빠는
신발도 못 신고 물기로 축축한 바닥을 성큼성큼 걸어와
떨어진 밥덩이를 주워 내 입에 넣어주었다. 손가락에
달라붙은 밥알까지 알뜰히 떼어 먹이고 나서야 신발을
찾아 신었다. 뭔 일이라도 잡아서 일당 반이라도 받아
올 테니까 먹던 밥 먹어.

"사람들이 너에게 일자리를 주지 않아도 빵은 주어야
해. 그래야 돼지지 않으니까."

화성빵집에선 여전히 오렌지색 불빛이 새어나오고
있다. 오늘 밤 어디라도 털어야 한다면 저기다. 화성빵
집이 가르쳐준, 빵을 구하는 두 번째 방법은 바지를 벗
는 것이었다.

그날따라 편의점도 빵집도 만만치가 않았다. 걷다 보
니 화성빵집 앞이었다. 손님이 뜸한 시간이어서인지 주
인 남자는 느긋하게 의자에 기대앉아 신문을 넘기고 있

foreigners: he was lending money to foreigners at an exorbitant interest rate, holding their passports in security for their loans. Although the Muslims said that they considered moneylending a sin, they couldn't help frequenting the bakery since it was the only place in Hwaseong that loaned them money. They might run away from the factories they worked in, but it was impossible for them to escape the bakery because of the passports they left in the baker's hand. The baker would report to the immigration bureau any foreigners whose interest payments were even a day late or who failed to show up on time. Once they were put under investigation and their passports were left unidentified, they were usually deported. So, the foreigners voluntarily reported to the baker. Even after they became illegal aliens, they still could not unfetter themselves from the baker. Even if they resigned themselves to the deportation, without their passports they would be detained in the refuge camp for foreigners for anywhere from half to a full year. No matter what, the bakery was their last resort.

The foreigner kept staring straight into the eyes of the bakery owner. The owner, undaunted, stared back at him. I thought that the crescent

었다. 지금이다. 주머니 속의 칼을 단단히 쥐고 빵집으로 들어갔다. 나도 모르게 칼날 버튼 위에 올려놓은 엄지손가락에 힘이 들어갔다. 찌륵. 카운터의 남자가 고개를 들었다. 눈이 마주치자 일이 더럽게 꼬여간다는 직감이 들었다. 천장 위의 바게트나 단팥빵이 귀에 대고 일러주는 것처럼 선명한 느낌이었다. 긴 요리사 모자 아래 도사린 남자의 눈에는 사람을 얼어붙게 하는 뭔가가 있었다. 남자의 눈빛이 머리 꼭대기에서부터 발끝까지 내 몸을 긁어내렸다. 되돌아 나가기에는 늦어버렸다. 어느새 남자가 등 뒤로 붙었다. 순식간에 벌어진 일이었다. 두 팔이 뒤로 꺾이고 칼은 남자의 손에 쥐어졌다.

"빵이 필요해?"

나는 고개를 끄덕였다. 팔이 부러질 것처럼 아팠고, 무엇보다 배가 고픈 건 사실이었기 때문이다. 남자가 내 바지 뒤춤을 단단히 움켜쥐고 끌고 갔다. 나는 넘어지지 않으려 뒷걸음질로 비틀거렸다. 남자가 진열대 위로 내 얼굴을 짓눌렀다. 카스텔라가 뺨에 뭉개졌다. 칼에 찔릴 수도 있다는 생각을 했지만 바지를 벗기게 될 줄은 몰랐다. 무슨 말이든 해야 했다. 바지를 벗는 대신

would penetrate the owner's chest at any moment. I closed my eyes. I could still hear the owner's voice:

"Take it and scram! If you show up here again, you're dead meat! I'll let it pass this time since I'm still in business thanks to you Muslims. I don't care what Allah says. In Hwaseong Bakery, I am Allah."

The foreigner hurriedly left the store after laughingly saying "Inshallah." I leapt aside to make room for him to pass. "Inshallah! Inshallah!" I whispered the word—with no clue to its meaning—at the foreigner's back. An obligation to provide bread. 'Didn't he say that people had an obligation to provide bread for kids like me?' What he said was not just words, but something that I could lean on—at least for me who had nothing and no one to rely on. Since then, whenever I had to use a knife instead of money, I reminded myself of the term inshallah, as if pulling a bill out of my wallet. Hwaseong Bakery was far from what I had imagined the real Mars would be like. But still, it was a bright star for me. It had taught me how to get bread in case I made up my mind to do it.

My method of robbing a bakery was a little bit different from the foreigner's. Yes, we both non-

오븐의 철판을 닦으면 안 되겠느냐고 했다.

"너 같은 애는 바지라도 벗어서 흔들어야지. 구조신호
지. 에스오에스."

남자가 크림빵을 내 입에 밀어넣었다. 딱 빵 한 개를
먹을 만큼만 대주겠다고 이를 앙다물었다. 남자가 내게
부딪혀올 때마다 진열대가 벽을 두드렸다. 탁. 탁. 타타.
탁. 도넛과 별사탕과 바게트가 둥둥 떠 있는 우주에 모
스부호를 보내는 것 같았다. 탁. 타타탁. 타탁. 탁. 탁. 이
쪽 벽에서 저쪽 벽으로, 천장에서 바닥으로 모스부호가
떠다녔다. 빵 우주는 꼼짝도 하지 않았다. 타. 타. 탁탁.
타. 타. 타. 모스부호가 어지럽게 빙빙 돌았다. 나는 빵
을 퉤 뱉으며 벌떡 몸을 일으켰다. 내 뒤통수에 면상을
호되게 맞은 남자가 뒤로 벌렁 나자빠졌다. 진열대 뒤
쪽으로 쪽문이 보였다. 문을 열자 좁은 계단이 나왔다.
언젠가 옥상으로 올라갔던 계단이었다. 계난을 타려는
찰나, 남자가 외쳤다.

"그런 곳에서 얼쩡거리다 떨어져 죽으면 나만 귀찮아
지니까 어서 꺼져."

모자를 고쳐 쓰고 있는 놈을 지나쳐 빵집을 뛰쳐나왔
다. 빵이 필요할 때면 언제든 다시 오라고 놈이 실실댔

chalantly entered the bakery. But after that, instead of demanding bread right away like the foreigner did, I would calmly peruse the display shelves and begin to pick buns one by one, never more than three. If the owner took a hint and yelled at me, then I would draw the knife, staring at him straight in the eyes. It would have been better if the knife had been a crescent dagger. But the knife I found in my cloth wardrobe was an ordinary cutter used to sharpen pencils. When I pushed the rusty blade out of its sheath using my thumb, it made a terrible, metal-scraping noise that gave me the creeps. If I could do the knife-drawing part well, it was as good as mission accomplished. Kids like me would do anything. All the bakery owners in the world knew that much. All I had to do was to slowly retreat, once more raising the tension in the room, and back slowly out the store. In most cases, the owner didn't call the police, since it was just a couple of buns. The owner would bellow at me, running after me madly. It would all end after I turned a few corners. I had learned how to survive on the street for ten days or even a month if I wanted to.

"You... say that I can demand what is rightfully mine. But... it doesn't make... any sense. Who... on

다. 건물 밖으로 나와 모퉁이를 꺾어 돌 때까지 놈의 웃음소리가 따라왔다. 나는 모퉁이에서 우뚝 멈췄다. 빵집으로 돌아가 진열대의 웨딩 케이크를 뒤엎고 먼지 속으로 달아났다.

놈이 그 짓을 하려고 한다면 찌마도 가만히 있지는 않을 것이다. 하다못해 놈의 다리라도 물어뜯겠지. 난 100원에도 바지를 벗을 수 있게 되었지만 그놈 앞에서는 싫다. 놈이 아니었더라면 나는 바지 벗는 법을 몰랐을지도 모른다. 나는 주머니 속의 칼을 꼭 쥐었다. 찌마는 영 내키지 않는 모양이다. 억지로 여기까지 따라오긴 했어도 빵집 문 앞에서 들어가려고 하지 않는다.

"네가 빵집 터는 방법이라도 알고 있었다면 벌써 나는 바지를 벗었을 거야. 네 방에서 날 재워주어서가 아니라 그냥 벗고 싶었을 거라구."

찌마는 오래도록 날 내려다본다. 휑한 두 눈에 실일음이 낀 것 같다. 가뜩이나 추운데 지금 찌마는 눈동자까지 시릴 것이다. 그러고도 한참을 더 망설인 끝에 마침내 찌마가 빵집 문을 열었다.

빵집은 예전 그대로다. 케이크와 바게트와 도넛이 천장과 벽에 사이좋게 떠다니고 있었다. 남자도 그대로

earth... will give me bread... for nothing? Don't you know... my situation...? I'm not... like you."

Unusually, Chima spoke haltingly. Perhaps he was gasping for breath, after having climbed up the hill. Or perhaps, he was trying to swallow his tears. Anyway, I gave him a fierce look. But Chima didn't stop there:

"If people... want to give me something... then that... should be a job."

"Nothing comes into your mouth unless you work for it." Dad used to say so at every meal like he was saying grace. Whenever he skipped a day's work, we skipped a meal. Our room door opened onto the kitchen-cum-entrance. One day, Dad didn't go to work and just lay in his room. I snuck in and rummaged through the kitchen. I had just eaten, but there wasn't enough to eat on the table and I was still hungry. I hurriedly put one spoonful of rice in my mouth. I was reaching for some water to wash it down when my father burst through the door. He was holding his tool kit in one hand. Perhaps he felt uneasy about skipping work. Feeling sorry and embarrassed, I tried to hide the bowl of rice behind my back. But the bowl slipped out of my hand and fell on the floor, rolling towards the

다. 빵 우주의 알라답게 입구 쪽 카운터에 떡 버티고 앉아 있다.

"너냐? 또 빵이 필요하냐?"

"필요하긴 하지만 지난번처럼은 아니야."

"그럼 남들처럼 돈을 내고 빵을 갖고 어서 꺼져."

"오늘도 돈은 없어."

이것 봐라, 하는 얼굴로 놈이 입술을 비틀었다. 남자와 내가 초면이 아닌 것을 알고 찌마는 어리둥절한 표정이다. 이쯤에서 끼어들 때가 되었다고 여겼는지 찌마가 쭈뼛쭈뼛 말을 꺼냈다.

"미안하지만…… 저희는 돈이 없습니다. 그렇지만…… 배가 고파요."

남자가 어이없다는 듯이 웃었다. 어이없는 건 내 쪽도 마찬가지다. 이래서는 빵 부스러기도 어림없다.

"에스오에스 같은 건 잊은 거냐?"

찌마는 고개를 젖혀 천장에 그려진 바게트를 한참 쳐다본다. 다행히 무슨 말인지 못 알아듣는 것 같다. 찌마는 내가 그렇고 그런 애라는 것은 알고 있을 것이다. 그래도 내가 아무 조건 없이 바지를 벗기를 여태 기다려왔다. 놈은 태연하다 못해 유들유들하다. 놈이 날 본다.

drain. A white breast-like lump of rice lay on the cement floor as if it had just sprung up. Dad walked barefoot across the damp floor towards the lump of rice. He picked it up and began feeding it to me bit by bit, saying, "I will find work, any work, and bring home at least half-day's wage. So, you just finish eating the rice." Having fed me all the rice including the grains stuck to his fingers, Dad put on his shoes.

"Even if they refuse to give you a job, they'll have to give you bread. Otherwise, you'll kick the bucket. Shut up and follow me!"

The orange light was still on at the bakery. 'If we have to do it tonight, then that bakery has to be the one.' The second method of getting bread that Hwaseong Bakery had taught me was to take off my pants.

One day, for some reasons, things just weren't right for any jobs. Not at the convenience stores or at the bakeries. I was wandering down the street when I came to Hwaseong Bakery. It might have been the slow time of day, but the owner was just relaxing in his chair, flipping through his newspaper. It seemed like it was the perfect moment! I tightened my grip on the knife in my pocket and

저 입에서 뭔가가 쏟아질 것 같아 조마조마하다. 찌마가 멍한 표정으로 나와 남자를 번갈아 본다. 나는 차마찌마를 마주 볼 수 없어서 빵 우주를 올려다본다. 바게트도 단팥빵도 고요하다.

"저 애가 바지를 벗는 대가로 웨딩케이크를 달라고 하더군."

활활 불이 지펴진 오븐 같은 찌마의 눈 속에서 북두칠성 도넛이 새까맣게 타들어간다.

단팥빵과 크림빵이 날아가고 케이크가 사정없이 내팽개쳐진다. 고요한 빵 우주에 검은 단팥이 튀었다. 태양 케이크와 부딪힌 크로켓이 바닥에 떨어졌다. 찌마는 머리통이 빵 봉지처럼 터져버린 것 같다. 빵집을 터는 방법 같은 건 완전히 잊었다. 당황한 놈이 크림을 밟고 철퍼덕 미끄러졌다. 나는 재빨리 놈의 코앞에 칼을 들이댔다.

"금고 속의 돈을 다 꺼내!"

놈은 요리사 모자가 바닥에 뭉개져도 속수무책이다. 찌르륵. 놈의 목에 칼날을 바짝 들이댔다. 빨간 물감 같은 게 흘러나온다. 너무 새빨개서 현실에서 일어나는 일 같지가 않다. 칼을 놓치고 말 것 같다. 허둥지둥 고쳐

went in. I had to pass by the owner to pick up the bread. Without even knowing it, I pushed the blade button with my thumb. Hearing the metallic sound, the man looked up at me. When our eyes met, I instinctively knew something had gone wrong. It was a very clear realization, as if the baguettes or red-bean-jam buns hanging from the ceiling had whispered an unmistakable message in my ear. His body seemed relaxed, but there was something in his eyes under the visor of his baker's cap—something that made people freeze in fear. He glared at me from head to toe. It was too late to turn and leave. I tried to take the knife from out of my pocket, but it wasn't easy. The man wasn't some pushover. I hesitated. As soon as I felt the man behind me, both my arms got twisted up on my back. It happened so quickly. My knife was already in the man's hand.

"You need bread?"

I nodded my head. My arms hurt, as if they were on the verge of breaking. And it was true that I was hungry. The man grabbed the back of my pants and began to drag me. I was staggering backwards, trying not to fall. The man pushed my face onto the display shelf. A castella was crushed under my face.

잡는 사이 놈이 칼을 낚아채 찌마에게 돌진한다. 찌마가 밀가루 포대를 던진다. 펑. 하얀 밀가루가 날린다. 푸른 천장에 샛별같이 빛나던 오렌지색 조명이 뿌옇게 흐려진다. 빵 우주에 새하얀 밀가루가 내려온다. 내 머리 위에도, 찌마의 머리 위에도, 놈의 머리 위에도 쏟아진다. 온 우주가 하얗다.

찌르륵 찌르륵. 놈의 손에서 소리가 난다. 찌마, 튀어! 찌마가 반사적으로 돌아선다. 뒷문 쪽이다. 찌마가 계단을 타고 올라간다. 놈이 바짝 쫓는다. 나도 정신없이 계단을 탄다.

옥상에서 놈은 찌마를 구석까지 몰아붙이고 있다. 옥상 가장자리는 겨우 벽돌 두어 개 높이의 시멘트 턱으로 둘러쳐져 있을 뿐이다. 한 발짝만 더 밀리면 끝장이다. 나는 뒤에서 놈의 다리를 붙잡아 넘어뜨린다. 헐레벌떡 놈과 찌마 사이를 막아선다. 바람이 널뺀지처럼 가로 세로로 날아다닌다. 옥상 아래로 뿌연 먼지가 맹렬하게 소용돌이친다. 찌마가 황급히 내 손을 찾아 쥔다. 어디로든 달아나려 하지만 빠져나갈 입구는 놈의 뒤에 있다. 종이박스가 하늘로 날아오른다. 오렌지색 빛발을 받은 먼지들이 별빛처럼 반짝이며 쉴 새 없이

The thought of getting stabbed with my knife crossed my mind, but it never occurred to me that he would take off my pants. Caught off guard, I asked him if I could scrub the iron plate in his oven, instead of taking off my pants.

"If you don't have any money, the least you can do is to take off your pants and wave them around. Use your pants as a rescue flag, you know! S.O.S."

The man stuffed my mouth with a cream bun. 'I'll let you have only one bun's worth.' I gritted my teeth. Each time the man pushed himself inside of me, the display shelf made a clattering noise. It was as if those doughnuts, star candies, and baguettes on the shelf were sending messages in Morse code to the outer space floating beneath the ceiling of that bakery. Clatter, clatter, clatter! From one wall to another, from the ceiling to the floor, Morse code signs were flying out into space. Rattle, rattle, rattle! The bread universe was finally still. I spit out the bun and jumped to my feet. I hit the man hard with the back of my head and he fell on his back. I could see a side door behind the display shelf. I opened it and saw a narrow staircase leading up to the rooftop. Once I'd used the same stairs to go up to the rooftop. I was just about to climb the stairs

솟아올랐다가 가라앉는다. 오렌지색 먼지폭풍이다. 나와 찌마의 시선이 교차점에서 황급히 얽힌다. 찌마는 애써 내 눈을 읽으려고 한다. 나는 살얼음이 낀 그의 눈이 위태로워 보일 뿐이다. 빵집 하나 제대로 못 터는 찌마가 이곳에서 살아갈 방법은 없다. 빵을 찾아 이곳에 불시착했듯이 또 다른 행성을 찾아 달아나는 수밖에 없다. 밤을 갈기갈기 찢을 기세로 먼지 폭풍이 휘몰아친다. 오렌지색 먼지들이 하나로 뭉쳐 사납게 소용돌이친다. 나는 찌마의 가슴을 힘껏 민다. 찌마가 뒤로 넘어가며 두 팔을 활짝 벌린다. 유영하는 우주 비행사처럼 찌마가 오렌지색 먼지 속으로 빨려 들어간다. 검은 밤이 펼쳐진 그의 눈에서 별이 반짝한다. 난간 위로 올라서 찌마에게 손을 뻗는다. 찌마. 같이 가. 먼지 폭풍을 타고 진짜 화성으로 가자. 난간에서 발을 떼려는 찰나, 발목에 뭔가가 감기는 것 같다. 갈고리 손. 넌지뿐인 쌀 봉지를 뒤집어 탈탈 털어내고 있을 노파. 빈 봉지에 피어나는 먼지 속에도 화성이 있을까. 놈이 내 몸을 뒤로 잡아챈다. 나는 바닥으로 굴러떨어진다. 아, 찌마. 불어닥친 먼지바람에 빵 봉지가 미친 듯이 휘날린다.

『표범기사』, 민음사, 2011

when the man yelled out:

"If you hang around in a place like that and fall off the roof and die, it'll be messy business for me. So, get the hell out of here!"

I ran past the man—who was putting his cap back on now—and out the bakery. I could hear him snickering: "Come again whenever you need bread!"

His snickering followed me even after I left the building and turned the corner. I stopped at the corner, ran back to the bakery, turned the wedding cake on the display shelf upside down, and ran away far into the dust.

If he tried to do that to me again, this time Chima wouldn't just stand by. At least, he would bite the bastard's leg. I had come to a point where I would take off pants even for a hundred *won*, but I wouldn't do it for that son of a bitch. Without him, I wouldn't have learned the survival method of taking off pants. This time, a couple of buns would never do for me. I tightened my grip on the knife in my pocket. Chima still seemed very unwilling. Although he had been forced to come to the bakery, he wouldn't go in.

"If you'd known how to at least rob a bakery, I

would have already taken off my pants for you. Not for a room, but because I wanted to."

Chima looked into my eyes for a long time. His hollow eyes looked like they were covered in thin ice. It was a cold day; he must have felt like even his eyes were freezing. He hesitated for another long while, and finally he opened the bakery door.

The store was the same as before. Cakes, baguettes, and doughnuts were happily floating together along the ceiling and the walls. The man was the same, too. The Allah of the bread universe, he sat commandingly at the counter near the entrance.

"It's you. Do you need bread, again?"

"I do, but not like the other day."

"Then, pay for it like other people and get out."

"I haven't got money today, either."

The man twisted his lips as if to say, "Well, what do we have here?" Chima, realizing that the man and I had met before, looked around bewilderingly. He seemed to realize that it was time for him to step in. He began talking sheepishly.

"We're sorry that we don't have any money. But we're hungry."

The man, flabbergasted, burst into laughter. I was

flabbergasted myself, too. This way, we would get nothing, not even bread crumbs.

"This time, there's no S.O.S.?"

Chima turned his head up and looked up at the drawing of baguettes on the ceiling. Luckily, he didn't seem to understand what we were talking about. Chima probably already knew what kind of a girl I was. Nevertheless, he had been waiting for me to take off my pants unconditionally. The owner was not only nonchalant, but also cheeky, tenaciously looking straight into my eyes. I was worried that some words might gush out of that mouth of his. Chima looked at me and then the man, his eyes going back and forth between us again and again. Unable to look Chima in the face, I looked up at the bread universe. It was out of character for me to avert my eyes. Chima kept asking me what had happened. The baguettes and red-bean-jam buns were silent, too.

"That girl wasn't satisfied with one bun, and she demanded that I exchange it for a wedding cake."

The bread Great Dipper reflected in Chima's eyes was in flames. He realized everything in an instant, as if the baguettes and red-bean-jam buns had just informed him. A monstrous scream burst out of

Chima's mouth. Bags of red-bean-jam and cream buns flew all over; he began to fling cakes violently down onto the floor. Chima's head seemed to burst open like one of those bags of buns. The tranquil bread universe was spattered all over with dark red bean paste. Croquettes bounced off of the cake sun and fell to the floor. The bastard was getting so flustered that he slipped on cake cream and fell down. Chima had completely forgotten all his how-to-rob-a-bakery lessons. I flipped the blade out at the baker's nose.

"Take out all the money in the cash register."

It didn't sound like my own voice. The words seemed to march out of my throat stiffly. The son of a bitch was watching his trampled baker's cap on the floor, not knowing what to do about it. I put the blade right up to the skin of his neck, just to scare him. Red ink-like liquid flowed out. It was much too red to be real. I thought that the knife might slip and I tried to get a fresh grip on it. For a second, that thought distracted me. The bastard didn't lose his chance and snatched the knife from my hand. Before I could do anything, he rushed to Chima, who had been thrashing anything he could get his hands on. At the sight of the baker coming at him, Chima, surprised, threw a bag of flour at him. The bag burst and white flour particles floated and spread through the air. The orange light that used to shine like the morning star against the blue ceiling was now blurred and dim. The bread universe was covered in white flour.

The flour-covered bastard looked like a snowman. Suddenly, I heard a metallic noise. It came from the snowman's hand. "Chima, split!" Chima instantly reacted by turning towards me. Then, he ran towards the side door and started to climb the stairs. The snowman was right behind him. I followed them up the stairs, too. On the rooftop, the bastard had already cornered Chima. The edge of the rooftop only had a low cement curb, as low as two layers of bricks. One more step backwards, Chima would fall. From behind, I dove at the bastard's legs and he fell. I barely had time to put myself between Chima and the man.

The wind was blowing in every direction. Down below the rooftop billowed murky dust particles sparking in the orange light. Chima grabbed my hand. We wanted to run away, but the exit was behind the man. Paper boxes were blowing up in the air. The orange dust was twinkling like the stars, surging up and then down again. Dust storm! Chima and my eyes met. Chima was trying hard to read my mind, but I was just scared for his ice-covered eyes. I gripped Chima's hand with all my might. There was no way for Chima to survive here—Chima wasn't even capable of robbing a bakery. He had crashed on to this planet looking for bread. But now he had no choice but to flee and look for some other planet to live.

A dust storm was sweeping across the night, determined to rip it to pieces. Orange particles had clustered together and began to whirl around fiercely. The bastard pounced on Chima. "Run!" I twisted my hand out of Chima's grip and pushed him hard in his chest. Chima lost his balance. In an effort to steady himself, he took a step back. At that moment, his leg caught on the cement curb and he fell off. He fell with his arms stretched out. Like an astronaut bounding through space, he was sucked into the orange dust. In his eyes spread the dark night and a lone star sparkled. I stepped onto the curb and stretched my hands out towards where Chima had fallen.

"Chima, take me with you. Let's ride the dust storm to the real Mars tonight."

I was about to jump off, but something wrapped around my ankles. Hook-like claws. 'By now, the old woman is probably turning the empty rice bag inside out for the last few grains of rice. Is there a Mars, too, in that puff of dust rising from that empty bag of rice?' The bastard jerked my body backwards towards him. I fell away from the curb and back onto the rooftop. Ah! Chima! The bags for the bread were flying around madly as the dust and wind swooped down.

1) Hwaseong is a homonym for Mars in Korean.

Translated by Jeon Miseli

해설

Afterword

다가올 공동체의 준칙

이경재 (문학평론가)

이경의 「먼지별」은 선명한 이분법을 보여준다. 이분법의 양쪽 항을 차지하는 것은 '지상의 화성'과 '진짜 화성'이다. '지상의 화성'이 경기도에 위치한 화성이라면, '진짜 화성'은 태양계의 네 번째 행성을 의미한다. "찌마와 나는 지상의 화성에 잘못 버려진 거였다. 언젠가는 오렌지색 먼지 폭풍을 타고 진짜 화성으로 날아가고 싶었다"고 이야기되는 것에서 알 수 있듯이, 이러한 이분법은 '현실'과 '이상'의 이분법이기도 하다.

지상의 화성에는 공단이 있고 거기에는 "팔과 다리만 있는 것 같은 사람들"인 외국인 노동자들이 힘겨운 노동을 하고 있다. 화성 거리에는 개발이 시작되면 나올

Working Principles for the Upcoming Community

Lee Kyung-jae (literary critic)

Lee Kyung's "Dust Star" shows a clear dichotomy between the "earthly Mars" and the "real Mars." The "earthly Mars" in this story is city of Hwaseong, located in the Gyeonggi Province of Korea, as opposed to the "real Mars," the fourth planet of the solar system. As one might observe in the remark, "Chima and I had been by mistake abandoned on the earthly Mars. I wished someday I'd get swept up by an orange-colored dust storm and carried off to the real Mars," the dichotomy in the story also concerns the division between reality and the ideal.

In the earthly Mars, there is an industrial complex

상가 딱지를 노리고 지은 가건물들로 가득하다. 「먼지별」은 "딱 3만 원어치만 가르쳐준다"라는 문장으로 시작되는데, 이 문장이야말로 '지상의 화성'을 지배하는 절대의 준칙이다. 이곳은 모든 것이 철저한 교환의 논리에 따라 작동하는 작은 우주인 것이다.

무엇 하나 돈 없이는 얻을 수 없는 '지상의 화성'에서, 가출소녀인 '나'는 외국인 노동자들을 상대로 한 성매매로 살아간다. 어린 소녀가 이 험한 인생길에 나서게 된 이유는 비운의 가족사 때문이다. '나'가 노파라 부르는 어머니는 쉰 살에 아빠를 만났다. 술집 작부였던 '나'의 어머니는 아버지가 살고 있는 곳이 곧 개발된다는 소문을 듣고 집 한 칸을 가지고 있는 아버지에게 작정하고 꼬리를 쳤던 것이다. '나'가 여섯 살이 되었을 때, 어머니는 아빠 몰래 딱지를 뗬다방에 넘긴 후 도망친다. 노파는 10여 년 만에 거지꼴을 하고 집으로 돌아오고, 아버지는 노파를 보자마자 그 자리에서 죽는다. 이 비극은 돈만을 생각한 어머니의 탐욕으로 인해 연출된 것이다. 집에는 일용할 양식조차 없기에 '나'는 수시로 가출하여 공단 지대에 간다.

'지상의 화성'에서 교환원리에 따른 삶의 영위에 있어

where foreign workers, whose bodies seem to be "composed of only arms and legs," engage in heavy labor. The streets of Hwaseong are lined with makeshift buildings constructed only to get the commercial permits that will be issued once the urban development begins in the city. "Dust Star" begins with "I'll teach you... but only thirty thousand *won*'s worth," which is *the* absolute principle that governs the earthly Mars. This earthly Mars is a microcosm in which everything works in strict observance of the logic of trade.

No one can get anything without money in the earthly Mars. The unnamed protagonist, a runaway girl, makes a living prostituting herself to the foreign laborers. What forces this young girl on to her turbulent path in life is on full display in the tragic history of her family. Her mother, called "the old woman" by the girl, met a man at fifty. At the time, she was a hostess at a random bar when she first saw the man who would be the father of her future daughter. When she heard that the area where the man owned a house would soon be developed, she intentionally seduced him. Then, when her daughter turned six, she runs away after selling the residence permit to one of the "on-the-fly" real-

예외적인 존재가 한 명 있으니, 그는 파키스탄에서 온 외국인 노동자 찌마이다. 찌마는 '나'가 접근했을 때, 아무런 대가도 없이 3만 원을 건네준다. '나'가 끊임없이 찌마에게 3만 원어치 뭐라도 해줘야 한다고 생각하는 이유는, 찌마에게 3만 원을 받고도 바지를 내리지 않아도 되었기 때문이다. "돈을 주면 뭐든지 가질 수 있고, 뭐든 가지려면 돈을 주어야 한다는 원칙"에서 벗어난 유일한 사람이 찌마인 것이다. 이후에도 찌마는 바지를 벗기지 않고도 '나'를 여러 차례 재워준다. 이곳의 절대 준칙인 교환의 원리에서 벗어난 존재이기에 찌마는 제 입에 넣을 빵 한쪽 구하지 못한다.

찌마는 파키스탄에서 대학까지 나왔지만 빵을 찾아 화성까지 왔다. 처음 화성은 찌마에게 "지상에서는 찾을 수 없는 것들이 찾아질 것 같"은 이상적인 곳으로 받아들여진다. 찌마는 화성이라는 도시가 한국말로 태양계의 네 번째 행성과 발음이 같다는 걸 알고, 한국행 비행기를 타게 된 것이다. 그러나 '지상의 화성'은 '진짜 화성'과는 너무나도 거리가 먼 곳이다. 알루미늄 기둥에 손목이 깔리는 사고를 당한 이후로 화성 일대에서 찌마를 받아주는 곳은 없다. 어쩌다 일자리를 구하게 되어

estate agents behind her husband's back. The old woman returns home gray-haired and disheveled ten years later; and upon seeing the old woman, the girl's father dies on the spot. The old woman's greed is what brings about their family's tragedy. Having nothing to eat at home, the unnamed protagonist frequently runs away from home to go to the industrial complex.

There is one person who is an exception to the trade-or-die lifestyle of the "earthly Mars," a foreign worker from Pakistan named Chima. When approached by the protagonist, Chima gives her 30,000 *won* and expects nothing from her in return. Since the protagonist does not have to take off her pants for the 30,000 *won*, she keeps trying to do something worth the money for him. But even after their first encounter, Chima continues providing her with a room to sleep in, demanding nothing in exchange. As a being outside the absolute working principle of trade, Chima cannot even get a piece of bread to eat.

Chima is a university graduate from Pakistan, but comes all the way to Hwaseong in search of food. At first, Chima considered Hwaseong an ideal place where he could "find things that" are "impossible to

도 공장주들은 월급을 체불하기 일쑤이다. 이로 인해 찌마는 파키스탄을 떠난 지 5년이 지났지만 비닐하우스나 컨테이너 박스 하나 구하지 못하고 고시원에서 생활한다. 그 돈마저 떨어져 고시원에서 쫓겨나는 지경에 이른다.

이제 '나'는 찌마에게 빵을 구하는 방법을 가르쳐주기 위해 화성빵집으로 향한다. 화성빵집은 '지상의 화성'을 움직이는 교환논리가 가장 적나라하게 압축시켜놓은 공간이다. 그곳은 '진짜 화성'처럼 오렌지색 할로겐 등이 천장 위에서 빛나고, 먼지가 금박지처럼 반짝반짝 떠다닌다. 온갖 빵으로 가득한 풍요의 공간이지만, 돈이 없이는 결코 단 한 조각의 빵도 사람들에게 주어지지 않는다. '나'가 그 어린 나이에 성매매에 나선 것도, 빵 두어 개를 훔치려다가 빵집 주인에게 성폭행을 당한 일이 계기가 되어서였다. '나'는 단돈 100원도 그저 주어질 수 없음을, 가진 것이 없으면 바지라도 내려야 한다는 것을 빵집 주인에게 배운 것이다. 빵집 주인은 외국인들에게 여권을 담보로 맡고 터무니없는 이자로 돈을 빌려주기도 한다.

이처럼 자본의 논리를 미메시스한 강력한 빵집 주인

find here on the earth." When he learns that the name of the city, Hwaseong, is pronounced the same as that of the fourth planet of the solar system, he boards a plane to Korea. However, the "earthly Mars" is literally worlds apart from the "real Mars." After he is injured at work when a falling aluminum beam hits him on the wrist, Chima cannot get any job in Hwaseong. And even If he is lucky to find one, the factory owners delay his wages. Thus, Chima is unable to even acquire a cheap vinyl house or a container box to live in even five years after he leaves Pakistan for Hwaseong. He stays in one of the *gosiwon* box-rooms, but is eventually evicted when he can no longer pay rent.

The protagonist resolves to solve part of Chima's problem, and heads to Hwaseong Bakery to teach Chima how to get bread without money. Hwaseong Bakery is the embodiment of the logic of trade at work in the story's Mars. The interior of the bakery, brightly illuminated with orange-colored halogen lamps, seems to the protagonist the "real Mars," and even the air's dust particles glisten like pieces of gold foil. It is a space abundant with all sorts of bread, although, of course, no one is

을 상대로 우리의 찌마와 '나'가 빵을 훔친다는 것은 애당초 불가능한 일이다. 어설픈 강도짓은 끝내 실패하고, 찌마는 결국 빵집 옥상에서 몸을 던진다. 빵집 하나 제대로 못 터는 찌마가 이곳에서 살아갈 방법은 없기에, "빵을 찾아 이곳에 불시착했듯이 또 다른 행성을 찾아"간 것이다.

이러한 찌마의 최후는 사실 예상된 것이기도 했다. 이 작품에서 찌마는 '나'에게 끊임없이 아버지를 연상시키는 존재이다. 아버지는 노가다 판에서 근근이 연명하며 죽는 날까지 앞날이 캄캄하기만 했던 것이다. "모든 것이 캄캄했다는 점"에서 찌마는 아버지와 닮았다. '나'는 흔들리는 찌마의 눈을 보며 아빠를 떠올리기도 한다. 아빠의 눈은 "살아 있기 때문에 살아갈 일이 불안"하여 종종 흔들리고는 했다. 그런 아빠는 죽었고, '나'는 "죽어버린 아빠는 지금쯤 차라리 속이 편할지도 모른다"고 생각한다. "배고픈 사람에게 빵을 주어야 하는 의무"가 지켜지지 않는 '지상의 화성'에는 가진 것 없고, 양심을 지키며 살아가려는 자들을 위한 자리는 조금도 준비되어 있지 않았던 것이다. "일자리를 찾아 행성처럼 떠돌다 이곳에 불시착"한 사람인 찌마와, "마땅하게 착륙할

allowed to have any without paying. Prior to this visit, the protagonist was sexually assaulted by the bakery owner when she was caught stealing several buns; it is this event that later drives the girl to prostitution. The protagonist learns from the bakery owner that not even a dime is given away; if she has no money, she has to pay for what she receives even if it means taking her pants off for men. The bakery owner also lends money to the foreign workers at an outrageously high interest rate, holding their passports as security for their loans.

From the beginning, it is impossible for Chima and the protagonist to steal bread from the powerful baker ruthlessly following capitalist logic. Their sloppy attempt at robbery fails in the end and with particularly tragic results: Chima hurls himself off the bakery rooftop. There is no way for a person like Chima, who is not even capable of robbing a bakery, to survive "here." So, he "flee[s] and look[s] for some other planet to live," as he has "crashed on to this planet looking for bread."

In truth, the end of Chima's life is predetermined. Chima is the one who constantly reminds the protagonist of her father. Eking out a scant living while

곳이 없어 거리를 떠돌다 아무 데서나 바지를 벗는" '나'
가 나누는 우정은 현실적으로 아무런 힘도 발휘하지 못
한다. 그럼에도 그 슬픈 연대의 몸짓 속에는 다가올 공
동체가 지켜야 할 삶의 준칙이 오롯하게 새겨져 있다.

working as a construction laborer, her father sees nothing but dark days ahead of him. Chima resembles her father "in that they both reminded" her "of darkness." At times, the protagonist remembers her father when looking at the trembling pupils in Chima's eyes, her father's pupils often trembled as well. She ascertains the reason: "Because he was alive, he felt uneasy about making a living." After her father's death, the protagonist thinks that her father "might be feeling better now that he'd stopped living." In the "earthly Mars" where "the obligation of feeding the hungry" is not observed, there is no room for those who have nothing, and yet want to live in consideration of others. The friendship between Chima, who "wanders around like a planet" in search of a job "before he had crashes here," and the nameless protagonist who wanders the streets with "no decent place to land" and takes her "pants off anywhere they would have" her, is essentially powerless. Nevertheless, the working principles of life that the future communities need to observe are vividly inscribed in this tragic gesture of solidarity.

번역 **전미세리** Translated by Jeon Miseli

한국외국어대학교 동시통역대학원을 졸업한 후, 캐나다 브리티시컬럼비아 대학교 도서관학, 아시아학과 문학 석사, 동 대학 비교문학과 박사 학위를 취득하고 강사 및 아시아 도서관 사서로 근무했다. 한국국제교류재단 장학금을 지원받았고, 캐나다 연방정부 사회인문과학연구회의 연구비를 지원받았다. 오정희의 단편「직녀」를 번역했으며 그 밖에 서평, 논문 등을 출판했다.

Jeon Miseli is graduate from the Graduate School of Simultaneous Interpretation, Hankuk University of Foreign Studies and received her M.L.S. (School of Library and Archival Science), M.A. (Dept. of Asian Studies) and Ph.D. (Programme of Comparative Literature) at the University of British Columbia, Canada. She taught as an instructor in the Dept. of Asian Studies and worked as a reference librarian at the Asian Library, UBC. She was awarded the Korea Foundation Scholarship for Graduate Students in 2000. Her publications include the translation "Weaver Woman"(*Acta Koreana*, Vol. 6, No. 2, July 2003) from the original short story "Chingnyeo"(1970) written by Oh Jung-hee.

감수 **전승희, 데이비드 윌리엄 홍**
Edited by Jeon Seung-hee and David William Hong

전승희는 서울대학교와 하버드대학교에서 영문학과 비교문학으로 박사 학위를 받았으며, 현재 하버드대학교 한국학 연구소의 연구원으로 재직하며 아시아 문예 계간지 《ASIA》 편집위원으로 활동 중이다. 현대 한국문학 및 세계문학을 다룬 논문을 다수 발표했으며, 바흐친의『장편소설과 민중언어』, 제인 오스틴의『오만과 편견』 등을 공역했다. 1988년 한국여성연구소의 창립과 《여성과 사회》의 창간에 참여했고, 2002년부터 보스턴 지역 피학대 여성을 위한 단체인 '트랜지션하우스' 운영에 참여해 왔다. 2006년 하버드대학교 한국학 연구소에서 '한국 현대사와 기억'을 주제로 한 워크숍을 주관했다.

Jeon Seung-hee is a member of the Editorial Board of *ASIA*, and a Fellow at the Korea Institute, Harvard University. She received a Ph.D. in English Literature from Seoul National University and a Ph.D. in Comparative Literature from Harvard University. She has presented and published numerous papers on modern Korean and world literature. She is also a co-translator of Mikhail Bakhtin's *Novel and the People's Culture* and Jane Austen's *Pride and Prejudice*. She is a founding member of the Korean Women's Studies Institute and of the biannual Women's Studies' journal *Women and Society* (1988), and she has been working at 'Transition House,' the first and oldest shelter for battered women in New England. She organized a workshop entitled "The Politics of Memory in Modern Korea" at the Korea Institute, Harvard University, in 2006. She also served as an advising committee member for the Asia-Africa Literature Festival in 2007 and for the POSCO Asian Literature Forum in 2008.

데이비드 윌리엄 홍은 미국 일리노이주 시카고에서 태어났다. 일리노이대학교에서 영문학을, 뉴욕대학교에서 영어교육을 공부했다. 지난 2년간 서울에 거주하면서 처음으로 한국인과 아시아계 미국인 문학에 깊이 몰두할 기회를 가졌다. 현재 뉴욕에서 거주하며 강의와 저술 활동을 한다.

David William Hong was born in 1986 in Chicago, Illinois. He studied English Literature at the University of Illinois and English Education at New York University. For the past two years, he lived in Seoul, South Korea, where he was able to immerse himself in Korean and Asian-American literature for the first time. Currently, he lives in New York City, teaching and writing.

바이링궐 에디션 한국 대표 소설 050

먼지별

2014년 3월 7일 초판 1쇄 인쇄 | 2014년 3월 14일 초판 1쇄 발행

지은이 이경 | 옮긴이 전미세리 | 펴낸이 김재범
감수 전승희, 데이비드 윌리엄 홍 | 기획 정은경, 전성태, 이경재
편집 정수인, 이은혜 | 관리 박신영 | 디자인 이춘희
펴낸곳 (주)아시아 | 출판등록 2006년 1월 27일 제406-2006-000004호
주소 서울특별시 동작구 서달로 161-1(흑석동 100-16)
전화 02.821.5055 | 팩스 02.821.5057 | 홈페이지 www.bookasia.org
ISBN 979-11-5662-002-0 (set) | 979-11-5662-007-5 (04810)
값은 뒤표지에 있습니다.

Bi-lingual Edition Modern Korean Literature 050

Dust Star

Written by Lee Kyung | Translated by Jeon Miseli
Published by Asia Publishers | 161-1, Seodal-ro, Dongjak-gu, Seoul, Korea
Homepage Address www.bookasia.org | Tel. (822).821.5055 | Fax. (822).821.5057
First published in Korea by Asia Publishers 2014
ISBN 979-11-5662-002-0 (set) | 979-11-5662-007-5 (04810)

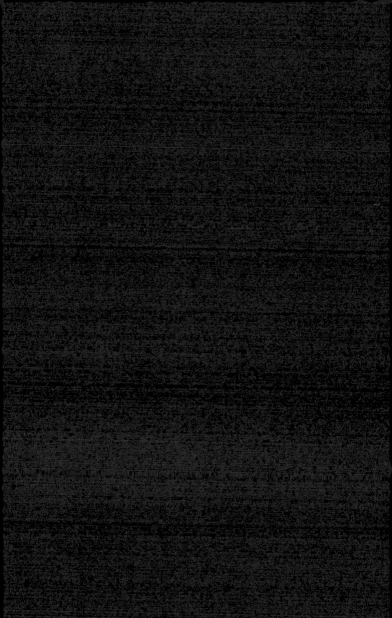